WILL'S BIG FIZZ

D1306165

WILL SQUIRREL'S
BIG FIZZ

For my family and friends

First published in Great Britain in 1996 by Sapling, an imprint of
Boxtree Limited, Broadwall House, 21 Broadwall, London SE1 9PL.

10 9 8 7 6 5 4 3 2 1

ISBN: 0 7522 0602 8

Origination by Loudwater
Printed and bound in Italy by L.E.G.O
A CIP catalogue entry is available from the British Library.

WILL SQUIRREL'S
BIG FIZZ

KATE VEALE

🌱 sapling

Will Squirrel is famous for his experiments.
This story is about what happened one day when
Will was making a special drink for Oliver Otter's
birthday. The drink is called Will's Big Fizz and
you have to be very careful when you are making
it because there isn't much difference between
the recipe for this drink, and another recipe for
making Fizz bombs!

No 19 **BIG FIZZ**
1. Large bowl cherries
2. 4 litres water
3. 8 spoons sugar
4. 4 drops lemon juice
5. 2 spoonfuls Extra Special fizz ingredient

No 20 **FIZZ BOMBS**
1. Large bowl cherries
2. 4 litres water
3. 8 spoons sugar
4. 4 drops lemon juice
5. 6 spoonfuls Extra Special fizz ingredient

Will was putting the last spoonfuls of his special fizz ingredient into the bottles on the kitchen table when the doorbell rang. "Hello?" Will called out. But when he got to the door, no one was there.

"Funny," he thought and went back to making his drink. "Now, where did I get to?" He couldn't remember, and put an extra spoonful into each bottle.

The doorbell rang again.

"Coming," Will shouted. When he got to the door this time he looked more carefully and saw Trevelyan newt hanging on to the bell pull. "Come in, Trevelyan," laughed Will and he helped Trevelyan off the bell pull and carried him into the kitchen.

"I'm making a special drink as a present for Oliver Otter's birthday," said Will. But he had forgotten where he had got to and he put even more spoonfuls of the special fizz ingredient into the bottles on the kitchen table.

The recipe for Will's Big Fizz says:

Be very careful not to put too many spoonfuls of the special ingredient into the bottles at this stage.

WILL'S BIG FIZZ

Will wiped his hands on his apron. "Finished!"
he said, and packed the Birthday drink
into his rucksac, put it on his back, and
then put Trevelyan on top.
"*Happy birthday to you . . .*" they started
to sing as they set off for Oliver's house.

Will, the bag, the bottles and Trevelyan
all jiggled along to the song.
The recipe for Will's Big Fizz says:
Whatever you do, don't jiggle the bottles
around in your bag when you walk.

"Digsby!" they shouted when they reached Oliver's. "What are you doing here?" "Hello," Digsby the Mole greeted them. "Oliver has gone to the Post Office to collect some birthday parcels."　He said he'd be back by 4 o'clock."

Will put his bottles of Birthday drink on to the table. "What is in your Birthday drink?" asked Digsby.
"Cherries, water, sugar and a very special ingredient!" said Will.
"Shall we try some quickly to check the taste before Oliver comes back?" asked Digsby.

HANDLE
WITH
CARE

LIVEN UP
YOUR LIFE
WITH
WILL'S BIG
FIZZ

IFE
WITH
WILL'S BIG
FIZZ

EX. SPECIAL
INGREDIENT
WILL SO. EXCLUSIVE

Will went over to the cupboard and took
down some glasses.
As he was pouring out the drink there was
a knock on Oliver's front door and Drew
walked into the room.
"Have a drink Drew!" said Will.
The drink had lots of bubbles. Drew took a sip.

Then . . .

HIC-

HIC-

HICCUP!

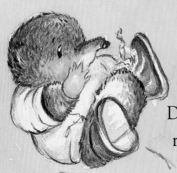

Drew bounced all around the
room like a little rubber ball.

His bouncing jiggled
the bottles on
the table.

Digsby and Will and Trevelyan all tried to stop
Drew from hiccuping but nothing seemed to help.

They ran up behind him
and shouted, "Cats"
and tried to scare him.

They got the cold front door key and put it
down Drew's t-shirt to try to shock him out
of his hiccups, but this just made Drew laugh
and he went on bouncing.
They threw a glass of water over him,
but this just made the floor wet!
They even tied some elastic on him and
dropped him from the curtain rail . . .

HIC-HIC-HICCUP

the hiccups came faster and louder.

With all the commotion, nobody noticed
that the bottles had begun to gurgle and
splutter and jump about on the table.

"BOOM"

Without further warning the bottles exploded. The whole room was covered in pink froth. Will had made Fizz Bombs, not Big Fizz! The corks became stuck in the lampshade. Trevelyan fainted!

"Oliver will be back in a minute!" wailed Digsby.
"We've got to clear up this mess or his birthday
will be spoilt."

They put Trevelyan in a bucket of water to help
him recover and then collected armfuls of pink
foam which they put in the bath with the cold
water tap running to wash it down the plughole.

The clock said two minutes to four -
Oliver would be on his way home now.
They worked even faster, scrubbing, wiping and
polishing to clear up the sticky pink froth, when
suddenly they heard the garden gate click.
"He's back!" Quickly they put away the cloths
and brushes and emptied Trevelyan, who was
feeling a bit better, out of the bucket.
Oliver came through the
door just as they
were drying
their hands.

"Happy Birthday, Oliver!" shouted Will,
Digsby and Trevelyan.
"Thank you," said Oliver. "Is Drew here?"
Before anyone could answer, the doorbell rang.
In walked Drew with pink froth on his head.
He had been blown right out of the
window when the Fizz Bombs
exploded. "Good drink, Will,"
said Drew without even
a hint of a hiccup.
"What is that pink
froth doing on your
head, Drew? asked
Oliver as he picked
up his Birthday
bottles of Will's
Big Fizz from
the table.

"Would anyone like a Birthday Drink?!"

THE END